Natalie B. Grinnell

A Japanese Journey

Volume 1

Natalie B. Grinnell

A Japanese Journey
Volume 1

ISBN/EAN: 9783337127886

Printed in Europe, USA, Canada, Australia, Japan

Cover: Foto ©Andreas Hilbeck / pixelio.de

More available books at **www.hansebooks.com**

A JAPANESE JOURNEY

BY
NATALIE B. GRINNELL

NEW YORK
UNITED STATES BOOK COMPANY
1895

LIST OF ILLUSTRATIONS.

A JAPANESE JOURNEY

FIFTEEN years ago a person projecting a trip to Japan was regarded by his fellow-men with feelings of wondering awe. He was a mighty traveller indeed, who had the courage and the time to cross the continent and toss for nearly three weary weeks on the bosom of the restless Pacific, in order to see that strange and far off country, at that time slowly and reluctantly opening its doors to the foreigner.

In these days of rush and bustle, of short vacations and exact plans, of vestibuled flyers, and ocean greyhounds, a trip to Japan is a very different thing. To the average traveller it means a swift rush across the country and fourteen or sixteen days of forced inactivity, while the stately white Empress or the huge Pacific Mailer, steadily ploughs her way across that immense waste of waters known as the Pacific Ocean. Then

A MUSHROOM CITY.

comes a bewildering, dream-like journeying from place
to place, each more strange and unreal than the last, so
that when one returns to the steamer at the end of four
weeks, it is with the feeling of having been thrown into
an enchanted sleep, from which one wakes only when
the long sea-wall of Yokohama fades away into the distance.

To the trip of which I am about to write, however,
belongs only the dreamy sense of unreality which it
seems to me must be left to everyone who has been to
Japan, under no matter what circumstances. Even prac-
tical business men going there on the most prosaic of
errands have felt the influence of this spell, which one
seems to breathe in with the air.

We left New York late in December, and after a
leisurely journey South and West, and a six weeks' quiet
sojourn in Southern California, we found ourselves in
Vancouver, B. C., on March 2d, with two days before
us in which to rest before embarking on the Empress
of China.

The air of the Far West is filled with the sense of

3

bustle and activity, and mushroom cities are entirely the rule. But Vancouver is entitled to a place in the first rank. Founded in 1878, it was slowly and steadily growing, when in 1886 a fire swept it from the face of the earth, only a solitary house being left standing. That blow from fate was all that was needed to inspire the energetic settlers; they went to work with a will, and in eight years have raised from the ashes a new city, which bids fair to equal any on the Pacific slope. In point of situation it is surely unsurpassed. Snow-clad mountains rise frowning and severe from the clear waters of Burrard Inlet in front, hills guard the city from the too fierce blasts of the North Pacific in the rear, and the harbor is such a fine one that the great Canadian steamers come to their dock at the foot of the principal street of Vancouver with as much ease as a ferry-boat entering its slip.

At 1 P.M., on Monday. March 5, 1894, the Empress of China cast off her lines and backed slowly out into mid-stream; then the screw revolved faster, and as we sailed swiftly between the pine-clad, snow-topped moun-

tains enclosing the bay, we felt a queer thrill of excite-
ment as we realized that we were really off for Japan.

Of the voyage, the less said the better. It was one
long, weary, round of bitter cold days, mountainous seas,
head-winds, snow-squalls, and dull gray skies. We were
most fortunate in having exceedingly charming fellow-
voyagers, and the officers of the ship were more than
ordinarily agreeable ; but even that did not entirely make
up for the discomfort of the voyage, and we were most
thankful when on Sunday, March 18th, we sighted the
sacred island of Kinkasan. Our first view of it was at
about eleven A.M., and we passed very close to its wood-
ed slopes, which are inhabited only by herds of deer. I
fancy none of the passengers slept very soundly that
night. I know that I did not, and day had scarcely
dawned when I scrambled out of my berth, and drawing aside my curtain peered eagerly out of the port-hole.
And then I realized that *at last* we were near Japan.
There, directly in front of me were the shadowy outlines
of Fujiyama, its perfect snow-clad cone rising like an
exhalation from the sombre hills about it.

5

Yokohama

THE sail up the bay of Tokyo is a most beautiful one, but there are so many novel sights close at hand that one fails to appreciate it the first time it is taken. Long before reaching our anchorage the steamer was surrounded by a fleet of queerly shaped boats called sampans, which are propelled by long oars wielded gondolier fashion, by scantily clad coolies. These men are very expert, and attain a speed which is surprising when one considers the uncouth shape of the heavy boats, and the primitive manner of using the oar. As the screw of the steamer turned more and more slowly, and finally stopped altogether at the C. P. anchorage, a number of bustling, panting little tugs clustered around, and with farewells to the officers and the few of our fellow-passengers who were going on to Hong-Kong, we carefully descended the gangway slung at the Empress' side, stepped into

6

the Grand Hotel launch, and were puffed and bustled off
to the landing-place or Hatoba.

We had been warned that it would be well to at once
declare our camera, so while some of the party started im-
mediately for the hotel, the Doctor repaired to the Cus-
tom-house with the camera, and I was left alone amid
my strange surroundings. The square plaza in front of
the landing-stage was filled with a motley crowd—Euro-
peans and Asiatics, Japanese and Americans, and in a
semi-circle beyond stood a perfect army of jinrikisha men,
bowing, gesticulating, and dancing in their excited efforts
to secure a fare. Amused and somewhat dazed by the
crowd and the noise, and the novelty of it all; I thought
I would step into a 'rikisha, and sit there to wait for the
Doctor, instead of standing in the sun. So pushing my
way through the crowd, I stepped into the first 'rikisha
I saw, and seated myself. No sooner was I comfortably
settled than the bearer raised the shafts and, to my hor-
ror, began to trot away with me. I screamed at the
man, and shrieked for the Doctor, but my cries only
made him go the faster, and I was whirled off around

the corner just as the Doctor rushed out the Custom-
house, and gazed frantically around to discover whence
came my despairing voice. However, my abductor bore
me swiftly to the Grand Hotel, and he was the only
'rikisha boy I employed during all of my stay in Yokohama. The jinrikishas are the first of the Japanese sights
to arrest the attention of the new-comer. Invented
some twenty-five years ago by a clever American sailor,
they have become a part of Japan. They are low, one-
seated vehicles, resting on two wheels, and with a pair
of shafts in which stands a coolie instead of a horse.
During the winter the costume of a jinrikisha boy consists of a pair of dark blue, skin tight knee-breeches, a dark
blue shirt, a mushroom shaped hat of canvas, and a pair
of sandals. During the summer almost all of this costume
is dispensed with—a breech-cloth and a pair of straw sandals being all that the perspiring bearers can endure. The
sandals (*waruji*) are made of rice-straw, and are so inex-
pensive that when they wear out they are simply cast
aside in the street, and the coolie runs barefoot until he
reaches a sandal-shop where his loss can be replaced.

9

In rainy weather the *kurumaya* (*kuruma* is the swell word for 'rikisha) dons a cape of plaited straw reaching to his knees, and increases the size of his hat to such an extent that the 'rikishas seem to be drawn by a mushroom-topped hay-cock with two legs.

The city of Yokohama consists of three divisions—the Bluff or residential portion, the settlement where most of the shops both native and foreign are located, and the Homera, or native colony. A long sea-wall called the Bund extends along the harbor front, and instead of being disfigured by docks and warehouses, it is made most attractive by clubs, curio shops, hotels, and a few residences. Several canals divide the city into sections, and one of these canals passes close by the Grand Hotel. Crossing this canal by a wide bridge, one mounts a steep hill leading to the Bluff. Up this hill toil wearily the coolies, bearing brick and stone for the constantly increasing buildings, and their plaintive cry of "Hill-l-lda," "Hoy-y-da," as they strain at the heavily laden wagons, lingers long in one's mind and heart.

On the Bluff are the hospitals of the various nations,

a charming recreation ground, a convent, and the residences of almost all of the foreign inhabitants of Yokohama. These latter residences are mostly built like bungalows — long, rambling, one-storied buildings, set in the midst of beautifully kept lawns and gardens, and almost all have a superb view of the bay and ocean. Beyond the Bluff, on one side curves the horse-shoe of Mississippi Bay, and on the land side are the well-kept cricket grounds, and the enclosure of the Yokohama Racing Association. For three days during May business is at a standstill, shops and banks are closed, and Yokohama yields itself up to racing. The emperor often comes down from Tokyo, the streets are gayly dressed with flags by day and with lanterns by night, and the entire town is *en fête*.

The Homera extends for some distance along the west bank of the same canal, and is a most interesting street. Low shops, open to the street, line it on either side, and it is here that one finds the umbrella makers, sandal makers, tortoise-shell workers, wood carvers, and wholesale silk merchants, who supply the goods to the retailers in

JAPANESE TEA HOUSE.

Benten Dori, and Honcho Dori. On the two latter streets one finds the curio shops, silver-smiths, linen drapers, and venders of silk—all the myriad magicians of Japan, who charm your dollars from your pockets in such a gentle and fascinating way that it is almost a pleasure to be robbed.

In the larger shops, both curio and silk shops, there is a regular fixed price, which no amount of bargaining will lower. But in the smaller shops, making a purchase becomes quite a serious matter.

Whirling by in your 'rikisha, your eye catches the gleam of a silver chain, or detects an oddly-shaped teapot, which you at once feel you must have. A sharp blow on the shaft of the "riky," or the cry of "*Maté, Maté*" (stop, stop), brings your coolie "up standing," and you descend leisurely from your perambulator at the door of the shop. There you are received by the proprietor with manifold bows and bends and snake-like hisses. Then, if you are wise, you begin at the corner of the shop farthest from the object you desire, and steadily run down everything you see. You ask the price of a few things, affecting utter scorn and contempt when the price is mentioned. In this way you gradually work around to the desired object, and ask the price with as great an air of indifference as you can command. When the price is named, smile sarcastically, and offer just half. The proprietor will bow again and smirk, and hiss, and mutter that it is "impossible, oh! absolutely impossible," but in a few moments, as a rule, will accept the half price and be thankful to get it. In some of the larger curio shops, it may be necessary to smoke a pipe or two, and perhaps to come up in price a trifle as the seller comes down, but, as a rule, one should never pay more than half the price originally asked.

It is very hard for the stranger to realize that the life he sees is the regular daily life of the people—a life as natural to them as our shuttle-like existence is to us—and at first I was constantly reminded of Mark Twain's remark about the French: "They must be a remarkably well-educated people, when the babies speak French fluently." It seemed most wonderful to me that the Japanese could walk so swiftly and so well upon their awkward wooden shoes, until I reflected that it probably was equally amaz-

14

ing to them that I was able to walk on high-heeled
slippers. These wooden clogs, by the way, make a queer
clack, clack, which will always linger in my memory as
one of the characteristic noises of Japan. As they are
held on by means of a velvet strap, passing between the
great toe and the one next it, the foot is partially
dragged along instead of being lifted, and the noise on
the asphalt platform of a railway station, for example,
is quite deafening. It is not so bad in the open air—
in fact at times it is quite musical, and seems to form
a rhythmical accompaniment to the soft chatter of the
women and the shriller cries of the children. Many and
many a morning have I been awakened before daylight
by the clack, clack, clack of the wooden clogs, and the
merry voices of the women, on their way to the tea-firing
go-downs, and peeping through the shutters have watched
the long procession file by. They come many weary
miles, these poor women ; some walk eight and ten miles
a day, starting from their hovels when the first gleam of
dawn is seen in the East, and only returning when the
evening is bright with stars. The latest baby goes also

HOLIDAY GROUP.

bound on its mother's back, and over one arm is slung a wooden pail filled with rice—rice, tea, and raw fish form ing their principal diet.

The garb of the Japanese adult is very subdued in color, as a rule, and many of these peasant women wear a dark blue or drab *kimono*, and a white cotton hand-kerchief bound picturesquely over their smooth black hair. In rainy weather each woman carries a large, flat umbrella made of bamboo and oiled paper, and the clack and the chatter are as merry under these shelters as under the blue arch of the sky.

The process of tea-firing is most interesting to watch. Each long room contains three parallel rows of firing-bowls. These are large iron bowls, set in a frame of brick-work, and under each is a charcoal fire. The tea-leaves are placed in these bowls, and tossed and turned by hand, the women working for twelve hours at a stretch, almost nude, and in an atmosphere heated to nearly 100 degrees. They use first one hand, then the other, and as the Japan-ese, as a rule, have beautiful hands and wrists, the process is very pretty to watch. When the tea has been fired to

the desired dryness, indigo is stirred in to give it the
proper color, and it is transferred to huge sieves. These
are taken to another room, and shaken and turned until
the finer leaves are all sifted out. Then the coarser tea is
treated to another process to deepen the color, while the
finer is turned over to still another set of women, who
carefully sort it by hand, picking out all the long coarse
stalks, and finally putting the finest leaves of all into
tin-lined and zinc-covered boxes worth almost their weight
in gold. In former times the women worked with their
babies on their backs, but latterly a sort of open-air crèche
has been established in each go-down. An open court
is set aside for the babies, and here the mothers deposit
them when they arrive, leaving them all day in the care
of an elder brother or sister, and patiently resuming their
burdens when the day's work is done. The average pay
of a tea-firer is the equivalent of 11.4-10 cents in gold for
a day's work of thirteen hours, and yet these laborers
earn enough in their four months of work to support
themselves and their families during the rest of the year.

Our first experience of a tea-house (which is a very

18

different sort of place from a tea go-down) was the second day after our arrival. We left the hotel in 'rikishas soon after tiffin. By an unwritten rule of the road the 'rikishas always go in single file, the most important person first, and the rest of the party in descending scale meekly following after. We whirled and rattled out of the court-yard, across the bridge, and along the canal for some distance, then turned back, threaded our way along the narrow dykes separating the submerged rice paddies, ascended a steep hill with many grunts and groans from our coolies, and were finally deposited at the entrance of Tenabes' tea-house, known as the "house of the 100 steps." It occupies a commanding position at the edge of the Bluff, and is approached from the city side by a flight of almost perpendicular stone steps, which gives it its name.

At the door of the low, one-storied, paper screened house we were met by a chubby, smiling little *mousmée*, and conducted along a narrow matted passageway to a small square room, divided from the rest of the house by sliding paper screens. As soon as we were fairly inside, the little maiden dropped on her knees, and bade us wel-

TEA HOUSE OF ONE HUNDRED STEPS

come in many low, soft Japanese words, meanwhile smiling and touching the floor with her forehead. Then four square, silk-covered mats were brought forth for us to squat upon, and we were served with tiny cups of unsweetened tea and queer wafer-like cakes, which the little maid handed us daintily with chop-sticks. Each cake had printed on it Japanese characters which were supposed to be our fortunes. Above the sliding screens were hung pictures of ships of all nations, and the *mousmée* brought out for our entertainment an album filled with the cards and autographs of distinguished visitors from all countries. Having added our cards to this collection we took our leave—a group of dainty maidens smiling and bowing, and calling soft *sayonaras* to us as we went. This is probably the best known tea-house in Japan, as the uncle of the present proprietor gave official welcome to Commodore Perry in 1856, and it has been the naval officers' rendezvous of all nations since then. A silk store in the settlement is also conducted by these same Tenabes, and Kin-san, the mother of the family, divides her time between silk and tea. She is no longer young, but her fasci-

nating manners, her sweet low voice, her quick wit, and
her knowledge of the English, French, German, and
Russian languages, make her still one of the most charming women in all Japan. On a subsequent visit she
sang us songs in all these languages, playing her own
accompaniments on the *samisen*, and when we rose to go
her gentle entreaties to us to remain just a few moments
longer, ending with the soft *dozo, dozo* (please, please),
made us feel that nothing would be lovelier than to cast
from us all thoughts of our western home, and to remain forever like the lotus-eaters in this " land where
it is always afternoon."

One feature of life in Japan, and one of which it
seems I should never tire, is going about in 'rikishas
after dark. When twilight falls each *kurumaya* brings
out his long paper lantern, inscribed with his name and
number in many flourishing characters, lights the long
candle, and suspends the lantern from the left-hand shaft
of the vehicle. A large party of us went out after dinner,
a day or two after our arrival. With many shouts and
cries, and much good-natured rivalry as to fares and

22

precedence, the long line of 'rikishas got under way, and we clattered out of the noise and electric-lighted glare of the hotel court into the quiet and moonlit darkness of the narrow Yokohama streets. The soft rose-tinted lanterns swayed with the coolies' trot like pendulous drops of light, and the warning cry, *eye-eye*, as we turned corners sounded like the plaintive note of some night bird. We wound in and out of the streets, and presently came upon the watch, a queer, gnome-like creature, dressed in a long, dark gown and huge mushroom hat, carrying an oblong " lanthorn " in one hand, and in the other a long iron bar, with which he beat the stones to warn evil-doers of his approach. He stood aside to let us pass, holding his queer light up that he might see our faces, which peered wonderingly at him out of the gloom ; then we whirled around another corner—and, presto ! we were in fairy-land.

Imagine a broad, mile-long street, lined on either side with low one-storied shops, entirely open to the street, lit by brilliantly colored paper lanterns, swaying from graceful bamboo poles, and filled with a dense crowd

WRESTLERS.

of laughing, chattering, merry makers, and you have "Theatre Street." Half-way up the street were two rival theatres, on opposite sides of the way. Every few moments a long narrow curtain was drawn up with a rush, revealing to the crowd of watchers the backs of the musicians and actors, and the faces of the audience, rising tier above tier beyond. The musicians were young and pretty girls, dressed in *kimonos* of vivid red and blue, and playing on drums and *samisens*—an instrument somewhat resembling a guitar. As the curtain rolled up the musicians redoubled their efforts, the actors played with added vigor, and the watchers gazed with bated breath : and then, just at the climax, down came the curtain with a bang, and a ticket-seller rushed out and, waving a handful of tickets, advised those who wished to see the end of this thrilling melodrama to purchase tickets without losing a moment. No sooner did one curtain fall than the other opposition curtain rose, and so it went on for hours.

At one corner was an apothecary's shop, distinguished by a huge death's head. Just under this emblem sat a group of students with huge books spread on low stands before them. They rocked back and forth, tapped their foreheads, scowled fiercely, and exhibited all the signs of being in the throes of learning to the wondering eyes of a crowd of laymen, who watched them from afar with awe.

On the ground in front of the shops were rows of street venders with their wares, their goods spread out on long strips of cloth, and lit by tiny lanterns set on short sticks, and here, there, and everywhere surged the people, the clack, clack of the sandals forming a melodious accompaniment to their merry chatter.

On another evening we went through a different portion of the town—the *yoshiwara*—or section set apart for the houses of prostitution. The social question in Japan is a very large and very important one—a problem the solution of which many of the greatest minds have tried to find. I do not know why this question seems to have been more agitated in Japan than elsewhere, unless it is because the Japanese discuss openly and in the most matter-of-course way, habits and customs of which we only speak in whispers and with bated breath.

With advancing civilization the Japanese have given up many of their primitive ways, but even to this day, in the interior of the country, men and women bathe together as simply and as unconsciously as Adam and Eve before they ate of the Tree of Knowledge, and many things at which we shudder are to them merely matters of nature. The lives of many of these people, which seem to us shocking and immoral, are not so to them, because the immorality consists in knowing right and doing wrong, whereas they do not know the right, and should no more be blamed than a heathen should be blamed for not worshipping a God whom he does not know. In all the large cities, Yokohama, Tokyo, Kioto. Kobe—a certain section of the city is set apart for the houses of prostitution. This section is known as the *yoshiwara*. and is under strict legal and medical supervision. The inmates of the *yoshiwara* are compelled by law to wear the *obi*, or sash confining the *kimono* tied in front. and they are also required to keep within the limits of the section set apart for them, so that no one can complain that the sights or knowledge of the *yoshiwara* are forced upon

27

TEMPLE GATE

him. Whoever seeks it does so deliberately and of set purpose. Certainly this seems a step in the right direction, when one thinks of the night side of Broadway, or the shameless exhibitions of the London Haymarket.

On the night in question we wound through the dark streets of the business portion of the town, and finally crossing a long bridge, whirled into the glare of many lanterns. We passed through street after street of low two-storied houses, the upper story dark, the lower story open, but divided from the roadway by closely set rows of bamboo bars. Behind these bars was a clear space about six feet wide, of bare boards, and then came a long row of fairly pretty girls, crouching on their heels, dressed in *kimonos* of vivid red, blue, and green, stiff with gold embroidery, their faces powdered and rouged out of all semblance of naturalness, and their hair elaborately coiffed, and bristling with dozens of hair-pins. The sidewalk in front was filled with a slowly moving crowd of men, laughing, joking, and sizing up the points of these poor little animals, penned in the shambles, and exposed for sale like any other live stock. The streets seemed endless, and in each exactly the same thing was to be seen, and the motionless figures, and the set painted faces and staring eyes of the little *koros* haunted my dreams that night, and many a subsequent one.

One of the prettiest jaunts in the immediate neighborhood of Yokohama is the trip to Sujita, a tea-house on Mississippi Bay. Following the canal back of the Grand Hotel, and climbing slowly up the hill by the race-course, one comes suddenly out on a broad plateau overlooking the indented curve and dancing blue waters of the bay. Far away along the horizon a forest of poles marks the spot where the fishing fleet is gathered, and dotted all over the bay are the gleaming white sails of the smaller boats, and the sampans of the fishers who have remained nearer home. At low tide the rocks near the shore are covered with sea-weed gatherers and clammers, generally women and children, the former with their garments tucked well up above their knees, showing their sturdy, well-shaped brown legs, and the children dancing about, clad airily in their own glistening skins. Circling carefully down the hill, we run through a low, damp tunnel

at its base, and then come out close to the shores of the
bay, lined with the huts of the fishermen. These huts
are very low, and have long sloping roofs, covered with
a heavy thatch, and along each ridge-pole grows a row
of lilies. Tradition has it that some centuries ago, the
ladies of Japan made of these lilies a very superior face-
powder, and devoted so much time to the cultivation of
the lilies and the manufacture of the powder that their
households suffered ; so the emperor issued a decree that
the lilies should no longer be grown on the face of the
earth. Whereupon, the women promptly dug them up
and planted them upon the roofs, where they grow to
this day. In nearly every house were groups of women
and children drying seaweed, or drinking tea, or smoking pipes, or washing themselves, or arranging their hair.
The entire front of the house being open to the street, the
most minute detail of the toilet may be observed by those
passers-by who care to look ; but it is such a matter of
course to these child-like people that scarcely any even
turned the head.

Finally we turned abruptly to the right, rattled down a

narrow stony lane, and alighted at the entrance to the tea-house which was our goal.

The tea-house stands close by an ancient temple, in a grove of beautiful plum-trees, which are laden with blossoms during March. Tables are set under the trees, from the lower branches of which sway strips of paper covered with Japanese characters. These our guide informed us were poems written by different visitors to praise the trees and the temple. He translated one of them as follows :

" We know all flowers must fade, yet we pity that spring will be over."

An ancient graveyard on the sloping hillside behind keeps watch over all, and we climbed up to it, hoping to be able to find some food for the camera ; a crowd of children who had been playing hide-and-seek among the stones ran away laughing and stumbling over the narrow mounds as they ran.

One cup of the bitter pale-green tea was quite enough for us, and then we climbed into our 'rikishas again and returned to Yokohama in the cool purple of the sunset.

No one visits Japan without making a pilgrimage to Kamakura, and gazing at the colossal statue of Buddha —the Dai Butzu. It was our fate to make this excursion on a superb May day—a day when the sun shone from the rising to the setting thereof in a sky of fleckless blue —a day when the soft breeze that tempered the sun's rays was laden with perfume—a day when the song of the birds rang sweeter and clearer from the very rapture of being alive—a day, in short, when all nature sang and laughed and during which life seemed a very sweet and pleasant thing.

We left Yokohama at 12.30, and the fact that it was a children's fête-day at a temple midway between Yokohama and Kamakura, made our hour's journey doubly interesting. The second and third class carriages were filled with women, each with a gaily dressed baby on her back, and with from four to ten other babies toddling at her side. This carrying of the babies on the back is one of the most picturesque features of Japanese life. As soon

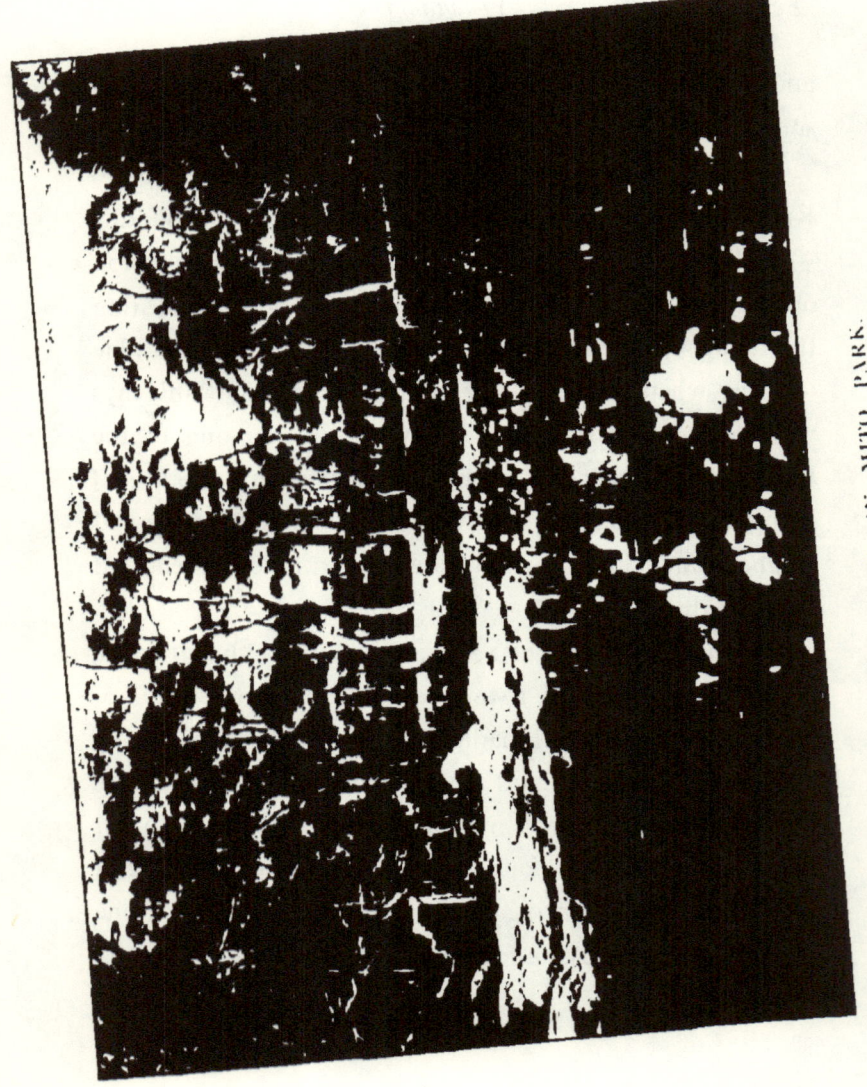

A CORNER IN MITO PARK.

as a child is able to walk, a large doll is tied on its back, and it carries that burden until it is old enough to carry a real baby, which is pretty sure to have arrived in the family in the meantime. The babies do not seem to mind being carried in this way at all, but eat and sleep contentedly while the bearer pursues the ordinary avocations of life, running, working, and even playing leapfrog with as little regard for the living burden as for the doll.

Though the costumes of the adults are as a rule very sombre, they give free run to the national love of color in the garb of the children. and on feast days especially they blossom like the rose, and in their *kimonos* of many colors, their hair elaborately dressed and adorned with cherry blossoms or roses of silk, which so closely imitate nature as to bear the closest inspection, they are most attractive little people.

Having reached the festival village and left most of our fellow - passengers to clack, clack along its shady street to the temple, we were able to turn our attention to the country through which we were passing. We

STEPS OF TEMPLE OF HACHMAN.

found it a very uninteresting substitute, as the road was lined on either side by the rice paddies, most of them under water, and divided by narrow muddy dykes, on which the half-clad, dirty laborers stood leaning on their mud hoes, and watching the passing train with dull and tired eyes. Every mile or so, a hillock reared itself above its moist surroundings, and gave footing to a grove of cryptomerias enclosing a temple, and now and then we saw a field yellow with mustard, or passed a bit of higher ground covered with pear-trees trained on a flat trellis forming a canopy to the entire farm.

Presently the train stopped at the tiny wooden station at Kamakura, and we descended to become the objects of a good-natured 'rikisha fight, *comme toujours*.

Matters having been settled in the usual laughing fashion, we mounted into our respective vehicles and started for the first object of our journey, the temple of Hachiman, the god of war. During the middle ages Kamakura was one of the military capitals of Japan, but time has done its slow and fatal work here, as in so many other Japanese towns, and rice paddies and wheat fields

37

have taken the place of fortresses and parade grounds. The once wide avenues have shrunk into muddy lanes, and the grand old cryptomerias which proudly waved their branches over the superb trappings of the armies of the Shoguns, now sigh sadly above white clad pilgrims, and inquisitive globe-trotters. The temple of the war god is but a fragment of what it was in those good old days when Shoguns, regents and heroes, accompanied by thousands of their followers, came to implore the aid of Hachiman before entering into battle ; but the small bit that remains is most imposingly situated.

A flight of fifty eight broad stone steps. flanked on the left by a huge tree twelve hundred years old, leads to a broad platform in front of the temple. The steps look very high and very steep as one stands at the bottom. but when once the top is reached one feels well repaid for the climb, for from the torii at the foot an avenue of cryptomerias runs straight forward to where the sea dances in the sunshine a mile and a half away. Inside the temple one is shown various relics, such as the sword of Hachiman and the helmet of Iyeyasu. which the priests touch

with reverent hands, but which to the outsider seem to
be merely very badly battered bits of old iron.

Having made the regulation round we set forth once
more, and made our way down the famous avenue, and
by divers side-paths skirting rice paddies, and winding
through fields of softly swaying wheat, to the little Ka-
hin Inn by the shore, where we lunched. The low two-
storied white building is set in the midst of a grove of
pines, which have been blown into most grotesque shapes
by the constantly prevailing south wind, and the soft
soughing of their branches makes a tenor to the bass of
the ocean breakers, while the air is filled with their sweet
and spicy perfumes.

The Dai Butsu stands a little distance beyond the hotel,
in a tiny valley leading back from the shore, and is one
of the few badly placed show-pieces of Japan. It is ex-
traordinary to me that a people with the wonderful artistic
instinct of the Japanese, can permit the approach to this
superb statue to remain as it is. To be sure, Dai Butsu
has met with many misfortunes, tidal waves have swept
over and destroyed the temple which originally protected

39

STATUE OF DAI BUTSU.

him, and earthquakes have very nearly shaken him from
his seat ; but that is no reason why his visitors should
have to approach him by a narrow winding woodland
pathway, which conceals all knowledge of his nearness
until they are at his very feet. Once face to face with
him, however, one forgets his environments. Nothing
in Japan impressed me in quite the same way as did Dai
Butsu. The guide-book tells us that the image is made of
bronze ; that it is so many feet high and so many feet in
circumference, and that there are so many curls on his
huge head, each curl measuring so many inches ; and
each statement seems a separate insult to the grandeur
and majesty of that imposing figure. The quiet face with
its down-cast eyes seems to me to be instinct with the
noblest teaching of the Buddhist doctrines, and to per-
sonify the peace which comes to him who has met his
temptations bravely, has done battle with them. and stands
at last the conqueror of self.

Having gazed at Great Buddha until his silent majesty
was indelibly impressed upon our minds. and having pho-
tographed him from every point, we followed a white clad

priest through a low door in the side of the pedestal, and looked up through clouds of incense to the top of the figure. At the height of the shoulders was a wooden platform crowded with gilded copies of the great original, and in front of us was an altar on which a light has been burning, and incense smoking, night and day for many, many years. And all around, on the green under-surface of the bronze, as high as hands could reach, were scrawled in chalk, or scratched with a knife, the names of many individuals whom the fool-killer has not yet had time to remove from the face of the earth ! So badly had many of these iconoclasts behaved, that at the entrance to one temple in Kamakura a board was nailed, on which was printed the following dignified and much-needed re-proof :

 " Stranger, whosoever thou art, and whatsoever be thy creed, when thou enterest this sanctuary, remember thou treadest upon ground hallowed by the worship of ages. This is the Temple of Buddha, and the gate of the Eternal, and should therefore be entered with reverence."

The day had been a long one, and we were all tired,

so when we had finally turned our backs on Dai Butsu, and found ourselves at the foot of a flight of steps almost as long as the ones leading to the Hachiman, and were told that at the top we should find still another temple, that of Kwannon, goddess of mercy, we were greatly inclined to take its beauties on trust, and turn our faces stationward. But Schimidzu, our guide, with his winning and imploring, " Oh ! please, you come with me—we go very much slow, I very much want you see this. This Goddess Mercy statue—very finest in Japan—you *please* come," at last prevailed, and on reaching the top we felt well repaid for the effort. The view from the broad platform in front of the temple was superb. At our feet was the village of Kamakura, with its two or three narrow streets, its heavily-thatched houses, and its acres of waving grain. To the left rose a range of rounded green-clad hills, and on the right the ocean heaved and undulated, gleaming purple and gold under the slanting rays of the setting sun. Removing our shoes, we entered the temple, in which we at first saw nothing in any way different from thousands of other temples. But after a low-toned conference between Schimidzu and two of the priests. we were conducted down a narrow passageway by the side of the altar. and into a dark Holy of Holies in the rear. For a second or two after the narrow door was closed behind us. we could see nothing at all. but presently, through the blackness we could make out the vague outlines of a huge figure towering above us, and gradually we became conscious that we were standing at the footstool of " Mercy." The priest, after bowing, clapping his hands, and rapidly growling out a prayer, lit two small lanterns which were hung on pulleys, in such a way that they could be raised and lowered at will, thus giving us Mercy in sections. as it were. The figure is heroic in size. carved of wood and covered with gilt ; many gold chains hang about its neck, and the broad, stupid face is surrounded by a crown formed of dozens of small gold figures. In one hand the goddess holds a medicine box, while the other hand grasps firmly the Sceptre of Power. It may be that Dai Butsu had absorbed all the admiration and respect which I could exhale in one day. or it may be that straining one's eyes through the darkness to see only

44

sections of a statue, is not calculated to inspire awe; but whatever the reason, I was very soon tired of Kwannon and returned to the temple proper, and there I found a dear, fat god, who will long occupy a prominent niche in my memory. He was a roly-poly, snubnosed, smiling deity, contentedly squatting on a lotus leaf, his fat hands comfortably clasped over a round and well-fed " tumpy," and he was painted a vivid scarlet. But his crowning glory was his cap. Some devout worshipper had bestowed upon him a knitted worsted baby cap, the colors of which would have made Joseph's coat sink into leaden-hued dulness. It fitted his round poll to perfection, and it was completed by a huge yellow worsted tassel, which hung down over one eye in the most jovial and rakish manner. Dear little fat, red-faced god, may your shadow never grow less, may the colors of your cap never fade, and may the donor of that cap never suffer from a return of the headaches which were doubtless the cause of its bestowal !

Dress, Manners, and Customs

I have spoken a number of times of the *kimono*, the national dress of both men and women in Japan, but have as yet given no description of it. The Japanese are, as a a people, so inherently ceremonious, that each fold in each garment has a meaning of its own—a fact which makes many of the natives smile quietly when they see the odd jumble of meanings which a foreigner puts into the wearing of the *kimono* and its accessories.

The indoor garb of an unmarried Japanese woman consists of a short under-garment of white linen, over which comes a long, shapeless garment of silk. Then comes a silk apron tied around the waist and reaching as far back as the hips on either side, and down to the ankles in front. Then comes the *kimono*—a shapeless gown of silk, silk crêpe, or cotton crêpe, with long open sleeves, reaching to the knees, and open at the neck. This robe

46

must always be crossed from left to right, as it is considered very unlucky to cross it the opposite way. A roll of colored silk crêpe follows the line of the outer robe around the neck, and then comes the *obi* or sash, which holds the gown in place. Great care is taken in tying the *obi*, as a few inches difference in the length of the ends, or a longer or shorter loop to the bow, marks the difference between the matron and maid. The *kimonos* are generally very subdued in color, but the *obi* is as gorgeous as one's purse can buy. Superb brocades, heavily woven with gold, silks of such royal texture that they would stand alone, crêpes shot with gold and silver, all woven in lengths of four and a half yards, are used by the rich ; and even with the very poor, the *obi* is always the most costly part of the toilette. The feet are encased in white cotton hose, reaching only to the ankle, with a digitated covering for the big toe. In the house nothing but the stocking is worn, but on going into the street the foot is slipped into sandals made of rice straw with two velvet straps crossing on top, passing between the big toe and the one next, or else heavy wooden clogs are as-

47

sumed, the latter making the musical clacking of which
I have so often spoken. The long, wing-like sleeves of
the maid are greatly shortened when she becomes a wife,
the white fold at the neck is changed for a colored one,
the loops and ends of the *obi* contract, the dressing of the
hair becomes more elaborate, and, worst of all, the pearly
teeth are blackened and the mouth assumes the cavern-
ous appearance which makes a married Japanese woman a
most hideous object.

The *kimonos* of the *geisha* or dancing girls are rich in
the extreme, the sleeves fall to the bottom of the gown,
and the black hair fairly bristles with gold and silver pins,
which stand out like a halo. On going into the street
both maids and matrons cover their house-gowns with
a long, grayish-brown cloak, which completely envelops
them : and in cold weather they wear a hood of silk
which hides all of the face except the eyes, and closely
resembles a Turkish yashmak.

The garb of the men is very similar to that of the women,
but it is almost always of a brown and black striped silk,
and instead of the *obi* they wear a small silk cord, through

which is thrust the inevitable pipe and tobacco-pouch. Both men and women make their long sleeves do duty for pockets, and the number of articles which can be stowed away in them is really remarkable.

One thing which always strikes the Western mind as very odd, is, that things Japanese always seem to work by contraries. The carpenter planes toward, instead of away from, himself, the needle-woman sews in exactly the other way. The builder makes the roof first, and laboriously builds the house under it ; the tailor makes the lining first, and adapts the coat to it. The horse in the stall stands with his tail to the manger, and the keys turn backward to lock. Many rivers are tunnelled under instead of bridged, and they dry up in winter and become roaring torrents at mid-summer. One might go on with these examples indefinitely, but after even a few weeks residence they become such matters of course that one ceases to notice them.

The politeness of the Japanese is proverbial, and is amusing at first, and then embarrassing, and even at times a little revolting. It is most ludicrous to witness a meet-

ing in the street between two men. They do not quite go
to the length of dropping on hands and knees, but they
bow and bow, drawing in the breath with a sharp hiss at
each bow, and when they finally cease and begin their conversation, it is a positive physical relief to the observer.
On entering a house both visitors and visitee drop
promptly to their knees, and bend the forehead to the
ground, hissing like so many serpents as they do so.
Then the pipes are produced, and the ever ready cup of
tea swallowed, and after this conversation begins.

Respect for the old is a marked feature in Japanese
life. The timid little bride oppressed and over-worked by
her mother-in-law, obeys the slightest wish of that person
without a murmur, hugging to her bosom the thought of
the day when *she* will be a mother-in-law, and free to
oppress others as she has been oppressed. The father
and mother, as a rule, work only until their children
are old enough to support them. Then they fold their
hands complacently, and submit with perfect composure
to being supported all the rest of their lives. The devotion of children to their parents is absolute, and when a

son marries the devotion of the daughter-in-law is no less marked. She becomes not only daughter, but slave, servant, and drudge, and unless she promptly furnishes an heir to the family, is often regarded with the utmost coldness and dislike. But time is changing the ideas of the Japanese in this matter, as in so many others, and of late years the condition of the women has been much improved.

When twilight falls over the city, and the soft pink lights of the 'rikishas begin to glow, there sounds through the streets a low, plaintive whistle that echoes like a pleading cry. It is the whistle of the blind shampooer, who steals forth in the twilight to knead and rub the weary limbs and aching muscles of those who have toiled during the day. These people are really massagers, and the profession is almost monopolized by those who are blind; and that it is remunerative may be inferred from the fact that some inhuman parents have been known to deliberately blind their babies, so as to render them eligible for the profession.

All night long their soft whistle sounds through the streets, and when day dawns they vanish to reappear only with the stars.

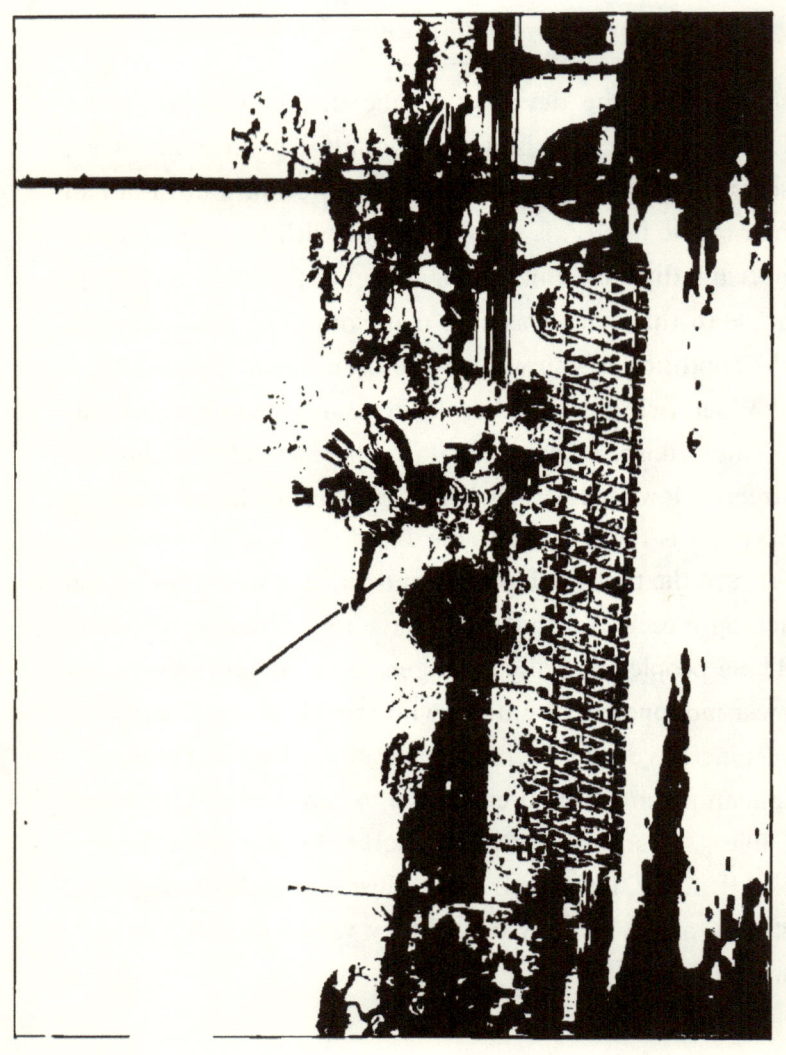

STATUE OF SAMURAI.

Tokyo

Tokyo, the capital of Japan, is at the head of the bay of Tokyo, three-quarters of an hour by rail from Yokohama. Here are the residences of the Mikado, the foreign legations, and two of the largest and handsomest temples in the country, second only to those of Nikko.

We saw it first on a sunny day in April, when the innumerable cherry-trees were just commencing to bloom, and the fresh new leaves were at their greenest. From the station we went to the Imperial Hotel, a modern marble structure situated opposite the moat which entirely surrounds the imperial palace. This moat is about fifty feet wide, and, on the palace side, rise stone buttresses overhung by dwarfed and spreading pines, and with massive guard-houses at every turn. War, grim and terrible, confronts one there, but on the city side peace rests on clouds of cherry-blooms.

CHERRY BLOSSOMS.

Having settled our belongings at the hotel we started
forth again, and short as our time in Japan had been, such
is the adaptability of the human mind, that it seemed
strange to find ourselves drawn by horses. Horses and
carriages are still so new in Tokyo that each vehicle
has two men, the driver and a running footman, called
a syce, who stands on a little foot-board behind the
carriage, and as each corner is approached, jumps down
and runs ahead to warn pedestrians to keep out of the
way. That first drive was a memorable one, for although
the number of foreigners is greater than in Yokohama,
the city is much more characteristically Japanese than
the latter. We rumbled through the narrow streets,
some of them so narrow that it seemed doubtful whether
the carriage could pass through, and finally came out on
a broad boulevard, which ended in the spacious plaza
forming the entrance to Uyeno Park. Crowds of merry-
makers were abroad, clad in their best bibs and tuckers,
wandering slowly to and fro, and fairly steeping themselves in the beauty of the cherry-blossoms. And how
beautiful they were! We drove mile after mile through

MEMORIAL TEMPLE.

double rows of trees laden with the exquisite pink and white blossoms. If we looked up it was to see patches of the blue sky through a rose mist; if we looked sideways it was to see the dark green of the tree-trunks through a network of softest pink; and did we look down, our eyes rested on a carpet of the fallen flowers. It was a very sea of blossoms, and one felt drowned in beauty. Satiated with cherry-trees we drove across the city to where the lacquered walls of the Shiba temple rose in a forest of dark and stern cryptomerias. No greater contrast could be imagined than that between Uyeno Park, with its cherries and merry-makers, and Shiba Park, with its dark trees and its silent temple, where the deep voice of a praying priest and the monotonous cawing of the rooks were the only sounds that broke the stillness.

I shall always have a tender feeling for the Shiba temple, because it was the first one I saw, and it seemed very magnificent then; but its glories were so far surpassed by the temples of Nikko that I have almost forgotten them, so I shall not speak of temples again until I

57

reach Nikko. Yes, just one I must mention, the temple
of Asakusa, also at Tokyo, and without a visit to which
one's memories of Japan would be incomplete. It is situated at the end of a long, narrow street, lined on
either side with shops, containing pipes, toys, hair or-
naments, hats, *obis*, in fact everything necessary for the
adornment of the outer man or woman, and also everything necessary to satisfy the craving of the inner one
from soup to *saké*. The temple itself is large, open to the
air on all sides, and reached by a flight of steep red lacquered steps. It is filled with a heterogeneous jumble of
gods of various kinds, imprisoned behind bamboo grat-
ings, huge drums, prayer gongs, and venders of paper
prayers. These prayers are purchased for an infinitesimal
sum, chewed up, and then thrown at the image of the par-
ticular god whom the petitioner wishes to propitiate. If
the little wad sticks, well and good, the suppliant feels
that his prayer has been heard, and goes away satisfied ;
but if it falls, gloom fills the breast of the unfortunate
pleader, and peace is not with him. From the rafters
overhead gigantic lanterns sway to and fro in the breeze.

and dozens of white pigeons flit in and out. occasionally perching on the beams to peer curiously down at the crowds below. The grounds around the temple are crowded with booths, and every day seems to be a fête day, for, go where you will, you are sure to find just as many booths and just as many merry-makers as the day before.

It was at Tokyo—but wait a moment. a matter so important as the Mikado's garden-party deserves a chapter all to itself.

APPROACH TO MEMORIAL TEMPLE.

The Garden Party

Lying in front of me as I write is a large square envelope. On it two names are written in English, and below are some Japanese characters. which I suppose represent the same names. As I look at it the familiar surroundings of this little New England village fade away, and I stand once more in the large room in the Tokyo hotel, where my eyes first rested upon this much-coveted piece of pasteboard. The windows are open. and as the breeze blows the curtains apart I look across the roadway, over the ruffled waters of the moat, made rosy by fallen cherry-blossoms. to where the massive stone buttresses and watch-towers guard the residence of the Mikado. This card that I hold is an invitation from that sacred person. who has so far broken through the clouds of mediæval superstition, that he is able to extend an invitation to this humble person from the little New Eng-

land village so many miles away—something which he
could not have done twenty-five years ago. though he be
" Son of Heaven, and Ruler of the Earth ! ! ! "

Inside the envelope was a square card of heavy pasteboard, bearing at the top. the imperial crest, the sixteen-
petaled chrysanthemum. in gold, and around the sides a
border of conventionalized chrysanthemums and leaves
also in gold.

The invitation was, of course. in Japanese. but it was
accompanied by a translation, greatly to my relief.   From
the latter I learned that

<blockquote>
By command of their Imperial Majesties
the Emperor and Empress,

The Minister of the Imperial Household respectfully requests the
presence of   at the Kwan-ou-Kwai (Imperial Cherry-Bloom Garden Party), to be held at Hama Riyu (Imperial Sea-side Palace) on the 12th inst., at half-past two o'clock P.M.
April 11, 1894.
</blockquote>

With this was a small pink card on which were printed
the regulations as to carriages, entrance to grounds, etc.,

and also the following sentence, which I have good cause
to know by heart:

" Gentlemen will wear high hats and frock-coats."

It was a command, you perceive, and I have always
heard that royal commands *must* be obeyed. The senior
male member of the party was provided with the necessary
articles of costume, but the junior member unfortunately
was *not*. As the invitations are only issued one day in
advance, there was no time to have the garments made,
so it was a case of borrow. One of our Yokohama
friends promptly came forward in the character of lender,
and promised to send the coat and hat by the first train
on the morning of the fateful day. So we went to bed
with fairly easy minds. Thursday, April 12th, dawned
dull and misty, and there were many anxious hearts as
we looked out upon the day; for be it understood that if
the day set prove rainy, there is no postponement " à la
Barnum " to the first fair day—the Garden Party simply
goes over to the next year. But as the day advanced the
clouds lifted somewhat, and by noon the sun was faintly
shining on the city.

The first train from Yokohama arrived, and the Doctor and I descended to the hall to receive the expected coat and hat. 'Rikishas rattled up and deposited their loads, the crowd around the door gradually melted away, and we realized with a secret chill that the expected bundle had not come. Of course, we promptly assured each other that we had not expected it by that train any way, and settled down to wait for the second train. The expectation, the chill, and the assurances were all repeated at 11 o'clock, and it was with a decided feeling of apprehension that we sallied forth to meet the third train, which was due at 12.30. A number of friends arrived, but no hat or coat. The situation was becoming exceedingly serious. The hat and coat were a *sine qua non*. Without them the Doctor could not go, and my pleasure would be ended. There was one hope left. A train from Yokohama was due at 2.05, and if the things came then, the Doctor would have just time to slip into them and be off at 2.30. The rest of the party donned festival attire, and then wandered gloomily about, counting the flying moments, and sternly avoiding any mention

64

of the faithless man in Yokohama. At last the train arrived, and with it came Mr. T's betto, exhausted and breathless, but with the precious clothes. Then came the getting into them. The hat went fairly well, but the coat—!! It hung upon the Doctor like a blanket. Despair again claimed us for its own, and we were about to relinquish the struggle, when the bright idea came to one of us to put another coat under the frock-coat. No sooner said than done—the Doctor's heavy Melton went on first, the frock-coat second. The fit was improved, but was far from perfect, and to cut a long story short, when we finally drove away from the hotel at 2.35, a stout and very warm gentleman sat at my side, securely buttoned into three coats, and knowing that nothing but a matter of life and death would justify him in unbuttoning the outer one !

The streets leading to the sea-side palace, which is situated on the bay, were filled with a very orderly crowd, gazing with awe-struck eyes at the favored beings who had been actually asked to look upon the sacred person of the Emperor.

MINISTER DUN'S GARDEN PARTY.

After a drive of about ten minutes we passed through a heavy iron gateway, and found ourselves on a gravelled plaza before the palace gates. Our cards were taken by an officer in uniform, and we were compelled to wait while he compared them with a long list which he held. Having satisfied himself that it was all right, he made us a low bow and waved us on. Inside the gates were dozens of lackeys in dark blue velvet coats, and knee-breeches heavily trimmed with gold, red waistcoats, white silk stockings, and low shoes with huge buckles. They conducted us a short distance, and then motioned to us to follow the crowd of gayly-dressed people who were slowly sauntering through the grounds toward a lake which gleamed through the trees in front of us. The walk was a long one, but the grounds were beautiful, and cultivated to a wonderful degree of perfection. The entrance reserved for the ministers of legation, corps diplomatique, etc., was divided from the other by banners of white and black silk, and lackeys were stationed at every turn, who saluted us humbly, but at the same time kept a sharp lookout to see that we followed the proper

path, and did not defile with sacrilegious feet the gravel
walk sacred to the Son of Heaven.

At last, after wandering through aisles of blossoming
cherry-trees, and under a long trellis already hung with
the pale lilac of the wistaria, we emerged on a grassy
terrace by the lake side, where we found a large crowd
assembled, and where we were told to wait for the appearance of their Majesties. The hour that they kept us
standing there was all too short, so absorbing was it to
watch the component parts of that very mixed assemblage.

How strange and unreal to New World eyes appeared
these Old World people! Unfortunately we were a few
years too late to see the court officials in their national
dress, as the Mikado in 1886 issued an edict ordering
the adoption of European dress for the state occasions ;
but the Chinese and Corean ambassadors, and a visiting
Indian prince, were resplendent in rich silks and brocades,
and the gay uniforms of the Army and Navy officers made
bright patches of color in the midst of the sombre black
coats and tall hats of the rest of the men. But as for the
costumes of the native women—! These queer, slanting-

eyed, black-haired, rouged little women wore the most hideous combinations of color, the most ill-made and badly-fitting gowns. That a nation so innately artistic as the Japanese should not have better taste when they don civilized garments, I cannot understand. Of course, there were exceptions to this, as to every rule, and some of the women were dressed extremely well in gowns that bore the stamp of Paris on every fold ; but the majority were dreadful ! Finally, after an hour's waiting the band burst forth with the national air, a chamberlain rushed through the crowd, forming us into lines on either side of the path, and the imperial procession appeared. They came across a long, low bridge spanning the lake, two guards first, then two court officials, and then the Mikado. His Imperial Majesty Mutsu-Hito, one hundred and twenty-first Emperor of Japan, is a short, bow-legged individual, with the slanting eyes, coarse black hair, and yellow complexion of his race, and on the occasion in question he wore the costume of a French army officer. He paced stolidly along, staring straight before him, one hand resting on his sword hilt and the other held stiffly

at his side. A few feet behind him came the Empress
Haruko. She is extremely plain — with very narrow
slanting eyes, a wee round button of a mouth, and
straight coarse black hair. She was beautifully dressed
in a pink brocade gown, evidently fresh from Paris.
On her head was a pink bonnet, and she carried a pink
parasol covered with exquisite lace. She is a tiny little
woman, and she walked with the awkward trot of feet
as yet unaccustomed to European shoes. But small as
she is, and ugly as she is, she is every inch an empress,
and there is a wonderful amount of dignity and strength
in her tiny frame. As she trotted along after her sullen-
looking husband, she bowed very graciously to right and
left, and even favored one or two exalted beings with a
pretty smile. She was followed by a band of court ladies,
and then we all fell into line behind, and formed a long
procession which wound along the borders of the lake,
and across another bridge, to the spot where the royal
pavilion stood on a slight eminence overlooking the
water. The pavilion consisted of a roof of thatch supported by bamboo poles, wound with ropes of evergreens

and camelias. One end was partitioned off by ropes of
purple silk, and partially shut in by heavy purple silk
curtains, and here stood the royal couple, while a number of presentations were made. The Emperor stood
near the entrance, scrutinizing each person presented with
sharp, earnest eyes, and after a bow and a few words,
translated by an interpreter, the presented one was passed
on to the Empress, who smiled graciously, held out her
hand to be kissed, and then turned away to greet the next
comer. Occupying the entire length of the main pavilion
was a long table very handsomely set, and as soon as the
presentations were over, the purple rope was lowered,
dozens of small tables sprang up like mushrooms on the
green turf, and innumerable lackeys served to us a luncheon which would have done credit to Delmonico. It
is whispered at court that the Emperor has welcomed
with rapture the advancing civilization which has enabled
him to banish from his table the raw fish, boiled bamboo roots, lotus soup, and *saké* beloved by his ancestors,
and substitute therefor the *pâté defoie gras, marinade de
dinde*, truffles, and that lightly sparkling nectar known to

the effete West as August Röderer, Grand Vin Sec! Be that as it may, the collation served under the cherry-trees at Hama Riyu, on April 12th last, proved conclusively to my mind that, though the Mikado may not always be correct in his choice of a prime minister, he can be implicitly trusted in the matter of a *chef de cuisine*! The luncheon lasted about an hour, then the living aisles were formed again, the royal procession passed between, in the same order in which it had come, and the Imperial Cherry Blossom Garden Party of 1894 was only a memory!

A Japanese Dinner

Almost the first thing done by the foreigner in Japan, is to partake of a genuine Japanese dinner. In all the large towns—Yokohama, Tokyo, Kioto, and Kobe—are Japanese establishments where dancing girls can be hired, and in this way foreigners can gain some idea of what a Japanese dinner is.

The dinners and dances given by the Maple Leaf Club, at Tokio, are considered the best in Japan, and it was our good fortune to be present at one. To make this possible, the men of the party had to be "put up" by a member of the club, just as with us. The members of the club are principally Japanese, but there are a few foreigners—members of legations, etc. We left the hotel at 7.30 P.M., and after a quick drive through the long, dark, mysterious roads of Shiba Park, we found ourselves at the lantern-lit entrance to the club. Two smiling,

73

A JAPANESE DINNER.

bowing little maidens met us at the door and removed our shoes, then we carefully ascended the highly-polished black lacquer stairs, and found ourselves in the banquet hall. This was a large square room, divided from the rest of the house by sliding paper panels. The floor was covered with squares of exquisitely fine matting, and the room was brilliantly lit by parti-colored lanterns hung by chains of unequal lengths, from the ceiling which was beautifully panelled in bamboo. At one end of the room was a recess, like a fireplace, containing a hanging scroll, called a *kakemono*, and a dwarf maple-tree, fully leaved. The furniture consisted of thin, square, silk-covered mats, and a large, dark wooden brazier, filled with wood ashes, at which to light the pipes, which are always *en évidence* in Japan, whether in shops, private houses, or public restaurants.

We seated ourselves upon the mats in Japanese style, that is, we crouched upon our heels, and the dinner made its appearance. The first things offered us were the pipes, which were duly lighted and smoked. Then, before each one of us was placed a square lacquer tray, standing on four low feet. On these the dinner was served. First came a covered lacquer bowl, containing a weak soup, in which floated small strips of boiled bamboo roots. Then came fish, raw and cooked, served with a pungent sauce called "soy." After that followed a seemingly endless procession of boiled meat, snipe, boiled lotus roots, pickled sea-weed, and the dinner ended with a dessert of sweet cakes. *Saké* was served all through the meal. It is brought in, in a porcelain bottle, which stands in a bowl of hot water. The attendant pours a little *saké* into a tiny, thin, china cup, from which one sips a swallow, and then passes the cup to his neighbor : said neighbor empties the remaining *saké* into a bowl provided for the purpose, the cup is refilled, and the ceremony is repeated.

When the supper was half over, the side panels were pushed away and the *geisha* (musicians), and the *maiko* (dancing girls), entered. The *geisha* were two—pale, tired-looking women, who carried their queerly-shaped instruments on their backs. The *geisha* are almost always women who begin as dancers, but becoming too old or too unattractive for that position, accept the position of musicians. There were three *maiko* — all of them tiny, solemn little beings, who seemed to regard their dance in the light of a very serious and important function. The *première danseuse* wore a very handsome *kimono* of satin, heavily embroidered, the sleeves just escaping the ground. The *obi* was white satin nearly covered with heavy gold embroidery, and a perfect halo of hair-pins stood out from her head. The other two were more plainly gowned, but all the costumes were handsome. After a few moments devoted to tuning the musical instruments, the dance began. Of course, the queer, slow steps, and stiff posturing conveyed no story to us, but it was most interesting to watch the earnest little faces of the dancers, and their entire absorption in what they were doing. It made no difference whether we watched them or not—the monotonous tum-tum of the *samisen* and the stiff posturing of the dancers went on just the same. When the dance was over, both musicians and dancers were asked to come over and have some port—the drink which they prefer to all others : so, with much giggling and many bows, they toddled over, and

77

having seated themselves in a semi-circle before their
hosts, consumed a tiny cup of port apiece. Then, em-
boldened by their libations, they began to inspect the
women of the party. They felt of the gowns, peered
under the hats, twisted the rings on the fingers. Finally,
when sitting on one's heels had become an agony no
longer to be endured, and we rose for a limping prome-
nade around the room, they surrounded us like a bunch of
talking flowers, and toddling by our sides, played at sup-
porting us as we walked, we, of course, towering head
and shoulders above them. When we finally descended
the polished staircase, and, having resumed our shoes,
were seated in the 'rikishas ready to depart, our last view
was of a row of crouching, dainty little maidens, smiling and nodding, and kissing their hands, while the soft
echo of their *sayonara* died away on the still night-air.

Kioto

Kioto, the ancient capital of Japan, is distant from Yokohama twenty hours by rail.

We left Yokohama at 12.30 P.M., having consumed nearly half an hour in packing away one large round table, one champagne basket of eatables, one market basket of drinkables, and two shawl-straps of rugs and pillows, in addition to the usual collection of bags, baskets, cameras, and umbrellas, which, like the poor, we had always with us. These proceedings were watched with admiration and interest by a crowd of natives, who measure their respect for the foreigner by the size and number of his bundles. The journey is through most lovely scenery. On first leaving Yokohama, we went through a section of flat, well-cultivated country, then the road followed the sea-shore for some distance, and then it turned up into the mountains, giving us constant change

FOX SHRINE AT KIOTO.

of scene. At first we passed for miles between the water-covered rice fields and saw the almost naked peasants laboriously stirring the mud with their uncouth and primitive instruments. The nineteenth century English railway train, as it rushed along the embankment above the fields, probably seemed to these stolid tillers of the soil as strange as their mediæval ploughshares and pruning-hooks did to us, and the contrast was certainly striking.

Kioto was reached at 5 A.M. on a misty, warm spring morning. As we came out of the station, dull and heavy-eyed from lack of sleep, it was almost startling to find ourselves in the midst of a merry, chattering crowd of people, on their way to worship at their favorite temple, before beginning their day's work. The long procession of our 'rikishas, on leaving the station, crossed a number of wide streets, rattled through a number of narrow ones, followed the windings of a swift shallow river through the heart of the town, and finally, after ascending a steep hill, with many groans from the 'rikisha boys, we were deposited at the entrance to Yaami's Hotel. The brothers Yaami were originally guides, and having become rich

through following their profession, they purchased two
tea-houses on the slope of one of the hills surrounding
Kioto, and transformed them into a hotel, which is one
of the best known in Japan. Unfortunately, the hotel was
very full at the time of our arrival, and the rooms given
us were far from comfortable, so after resting for a few
hours, we left and settled ourselves at the Kioto Hotel,
in the centre of the city. But some memories of Yaami's
will always remain—notably the soft booming of the temple bell close by, as it sent forth its silver call to worship,
at six o'clock on that misty morning, bringing at least
one Christian sinner to her knees, in gratitude for the
goodness that permitted her to hear it.

We were unfortunate enough to visit Kioto in the
midst of the short rainy season, and most of its absorbing
sights were seen between the drops, but they were scarcely
less beautiful for that. The first places of interest that
we visited were the palace of the Mikado, and Nijo Castle,
the former residence of the Shogun, and now the prop-
erty of the Emperor.

At the entrance to the Mikado's palace our passports

were severely scrutinized, and then we were forced to wait, while our guide changed the stuff trousers worn under his *kimono*, for a pair of silk ones lent for the occasion by one of the custodians of the gateway. Then we were handed over to the tender mercies of two palace guides, and were permitted to enter the sacred precincts. As we went toward the entrance for visitors, we passed a number of old women crouching on their knees, and patiently grubbing out from between the pebbles tiny weeds that almost required a magnifying-glass to be seen at all.

The grounds are large and handsome, and, as one may judge from the foregoing instance, kept in most exquisite order. The palace itself stands in the very centre of the grounds, and is a large bare building, almost completely encircled by kitchens, guards' residences, store-houses, etc. The rooms are huge, and furnished only by beautiful squares of soft matting, and gorgeously decorated gold screens. The room which the Emperor occupies even now, on his rare visits to Kioto, is a small square box, surrounded on all four sides by the rooms of his guards, and furnished only with a small elevated platform on which are thrown the heavy silk futons (rugs) upon which reposes the sacred person of the " Brother of the Sun and Moon, and first-cousin of the fixed stars." The throne is a low, red velvet chair, standing on a dais draped with China silk curtains, and having two red velvet cushions before it on which rest the hat and sword of state. The last time that the Emperor visited Kioto was on the occasion of the visit of the Grand Duke Nicholas of Russia, the present Emperor, whose life was attempted by a Japanese fanatic in Kioto, and saved by the coolness and courage of the Crown Prince of Greece.

The change from the barrack-like bareness of the Mikado's palace, to the sumptuous decorations of the Shogun's former residence, at the other end of the city, was most marked.

Having gone through the customary inspection at the entrance, we were permitted to pass under a massive gateway, crowned by a huge watch-tower, and found ourselves in a gravelled courtyard, terminating in a most superbly carved state entrance. Every inch of this is

wonderfully worked into all sorts of shapes of birds,
beasts, and flowers, and is only equalled by the magnificent carving at Nikko. The figures are heavily gilded,
and the leaves and flowers gorgeously colored, so that
the entire structure glows like a jewel. Passing through
the small opening at the side, one mounts two or three
polished lacquer steps, and finds one's self in a very riot
of superb coloring, which continues from room to room,
until one is fairly dazzled by the glory. The ceilings are
divided into panels, of which the background is gold
leaf, on which are most exquisitely painted an endless
variety of subjects. The walls of the rooms are formed
of sliding screens of gold, painted by the first artists of
Japan, and the matting covering the floors is of a pecul-
iarly soft and delicate weave. Everywhere, on the ends
of the tiny nails in the screens, on the huge bolts fasten-
ing the beams of the ceilings, on the borders of the
mats, in a never-ending procession on the divisions
separating the panels, even woven into the silken hang-
ings, one sees the three-leaved crest of the Shogun.
When the castle came into the imperial possession,

ON THE ROAD TO KINKA.

orders were given that these crests should be removed, and the sixteen-petaled chrysanthemum substituted in place of them. But the labor proved so herculean that it was too much for even Japanese patience, so it was given up, and the Shogun's crest remains, except in one or two rooms.

The number of temples in Kioto is seemingly endless, and the task of visiting them all would be almost like that of erasing the Shogun's crest. One of the principal ones is the Kiomidzu temple, the approach to which is up a steep hill, called Tea-pot Hill, lined on either side by rows of shops filled with cheap porcelain. At the entrance to the temple is a large stone basin, into which the water flows from the mouth of a beautifully-cast bronze dragon, securely fastened by a heavy bronze chain to a neighboring tree. The temple is huge, and open on all sides. At one side a platform, supported by a trestle-work of bamboo-poles, is built out over a precipice. From this platform, in the old days, jealous husbands threw their suspected wives. If they survived the fall to the jagged rocks of the mountain stream, hundreds of feet below, they were accounted innocent, and allowed to retire wherever they wished, to nurse their lacerated bodies and wounded hearts; if they were killed, as was, of course, usually the case, they were accounted guilty, and their names erased from the records of their own and their husband's families.

In this temple is the celebrated shrine of the Goddess of Marriage. The deity, a most hideous image painted a vivid scarlet, sits behind a lattice work of bamboo bars. The doubting maiden, and the timid lover come here, provided with long narrow strips of paper, which must be wound in and out of four of the lattice openings, and then tied in a knot, the thumb and fourth finger alone being employed in the operation. If any other finger is used, or even touches the paper or the lattice, the spell is broken, and the charm will not work.

Leaving the temple nestling on the hill-side in the sheltering arms of a forest of beautifully straight trees of every shade of tender green, we strolled down Teapot Hill, and turning sharply to the left, could not repress a cry of delight at the shadowy lane before us.

It is impossible to describe the delicacy, the cloudy softness of the effect, as we looked through the narrow opening between those lofty trees of feathery bamboo. The silvery lance-shaped leaves seemed to melt imperceptibly into the gray clouds above, and when they swayed in the breeze, it was like the gentle waving of a giant fan of thistledown. We walked slowly through the lane, steeped and enfolded in its misty, cloudy, silvery beauty, and rejoining our 'rikishas at the other end, rattled off to another temple known as the Temple of the 33,333 Buddhas! As one enters, one beholds a colossal statue of the god, sitting in state on the principal altar, while on either side stretch away, in endless perspective, life-sized copies of the great original, all in brilliant and unfading gold lacquer. A thousand images, in rows eight deep, fill the large hall, and the grand total is reached by means of dozens of tiny images worked into the large ones, wherever space can be found for them. It is a sight more interesting than beautiful, and the way to it was made dreadful by the groups of begging monstrosities at the sides of the road.

GOLD HOUSE AT KINKA.

A short distance from the centre of the town stands a
monastery, known as the Gold Monastery, from the fact
that the roof of a small building in the grounds is covered with gold leaf. We were met at the gate by a
white-clad Brother who made us sign our names in a
visitors' book, and then led us through room after room,
monotonously alike, and containing such imposing relics
as a tooth of the founder of the Order, his heart, securely
sealed in a wonderfully beautiful old Satsuma jar, a few
pages of the same gentleman's handwriting, etc. We
looked at them all, but I, for one, was much more in-
terested in our priestly guide, with his pale, ascetic face,
and also in a large pine-tree in one of the courts, which
generations of patient monks have trained into the perfect semblance of a Chinese junk. Our tour of inspection
over, we had the inevitable cup of tea, and then went out
into the grounds, which are justly celebrated for their
beauty. Standing on the steps of the gold - covered
building, which is on the bank of a tiny lake, the monk
clapped his hands, and then threw a handful of parched
corn into the water. In an instant the space before us

PINE TREE AT GOLD MONASTERY

was filled with dozens of fish of all kinds, sucking and fighting, and making the water fairly boil in their efforts to reach the food.

Before going to Kioto, we had been told that it was the Paris of Japan; that, beautiful as the embroideries, the carvings, the porcelains of Yokohama and Tokyo had seemed to us, those of Kioto would surpass them, and that, unless our resolutions in regard to the amount of money to be expended were adamantine, we would leave the city financially ruined. But in this respect we were disappointed. The shops were filled with exquisite goods, to be sure, and when the sellers found that they had buyers who were willing to pay for good work, but declined to take an inferior article at any price, they brought forth from the go-downs veritable mountains of silk, satins, and damask, embroidered most beautifully, but differing from the displays in other cities only as to quantity—the quality and execution seemed to us the same.

93

WOMAN'S FALL NEAR KOBÉ

Kobe

Leaving Kioto at noon, four hours in a comfortable railway carriage brings one to Kobe. This was the first treaty port open to foreigners, and, as at Yokohama, the city is divided into the "concession," where live the foreigners, and the "Native town," Hiogo. The latter is dark, dirty, and entirely unprepossessing, while the former, with its broad, level streets, its modern houses, and air of cleanliness and prosperity, reminds one forcibly of parts of Dresden.

Kobe is beautifully situated on a narrow plateau between the mountains and the sea. Its harbor is large and safe, and much more attractive than the harbor of Yokohama. The mountains which rise a short distance behind the town are of volcanic origin, very oddly shaped, and covered with a luxuriant growth of trees and underbrush, which gives a peculiar softness to their

95

strange outlines. We spent a pleasant week there, and then bade farewell to its quiet streets and busy harbor, and settled ourselves down for our twenty hours journey back to Yokohama.

Nikko

From the day of one's arrival in Japan, one begins insensibly to live toward Nikko. In each temple we enter, when a fine carving calls forth an exclamation of pleasure, the guide says, with a superior smile, " Yes, that is good, but wait until you see Nikko." From one's friends, from one's enemies, from one's tailor, from one's " butcher, baker, and candlestick-maker," comes the cry. " Wait until you see Nikko." until one finally begins to talk about Nikko by day. and to dream of Nikko at night. We were told that we had made a great mistake in leaving Nikko for the last. If so. it was a mistake for which I shall always be grateful, though I am quite sure that nothing could ever dim my memories of the enchanting spot. Our first view of Nikko, however, was distinctly unpleasing. Leaving Yokohama shortly after noon, we travelled through a most lovely country, and as twilight fell we began to ascend the steep slope of the Nikkosan Mountains. Our absorption in the scenery was so great that the unusually rapid coming on of night was scarcely perceived, until attention was called to it with abruptness and decision by a vivid flash of lightning, followed by a crash of thunder: and when we alighted at the small station, it was to find a very lively thunder-storm in progress—rain in torrents, and almost incessant thunder and lightning.

We cowered together on a narrow bench outside the station, cold, wet, and miserable, and wished that we had not come to Nikko! Presently the storm abated somewhat, so we decided to start for the hotel, which was a mile or more distant. We scrambled into our 'rikishas, the hood was pulled up and fastened, a cover of oiled paper was spread over our knees, and with three coolies to each 'rikiska, we sallied forth. That was just the chance the storm had been waiting for! The rain almost ceased, as the demon who regulates the weather at Nikko threw his head back and took a long breath, and then

—words fail me! It did not rain—no, all the waters in all the clouds in space seemed to have been piled up in one spot somewhere just above Nikko, and when the demon pulled the string, they fell in a solid mass that extinguished in a second our flimsy paper lanterns, bent the hoods of the 'rikishas in, wet us to the skin, and transformed the long, sloping main street of Nikko into a roaring torrent. The thunder and lightning were incessant and were blinding, deafening, and most terrifying—even to the coolies, accustomed as they are to the fierce storms of the mountains. But we kept on, the men calling and groaning as they pushed and dragged us up the steep hill, seeming to find their way by intuition, for the darkness between the flashes was the very blackness of darkness. The journey seemed endless, but at last we saw the gleam of an earthly light in the distance, and we presently rumbled into the courtyard of the dear little Nikko hotel. A half-dozen gaily dressed little *nesans* rushed out to meet us, seized our bags and bundles, and bustled us off to our rooms. Then they vanished, to reappear in a few minutes, blushing and giggling, and staggering under the weight of our trunks, which they carried swung from a pole resting on the shoulders. And when, an hour later, we found ourselves warm, dry, and "comforted with food and wine," we could look back to that horrible trip up as after all not so bad !

The meaning of the word Nikko is "Sun's Brightness," and despite our stormy experience on arriving, when we awoke the next morning we could not but feel that the title was well deserved. Our sleep was sound, as may be imagined, and it was some hours after sunrise when I threw open the shutters and stepped out on the balcony encircling the second story of the hotel. The day was cloudless and warm, filled with a thousand sweet spring odors, and the penetrating, damp fragrance of the rain-soaked grass. Across the valley rose the graduated slopes of the Nikkosan Mountains, covered with a growth of tenderest green, and looking a fit habitation for the hosts of sprites and fays with which the Japanese fairy tales people them.

Through the heart of the valley rushed and roared the

swollen torrent of the Diagawa River, and in the immediate foreground was the garden of the hotel, with its miniature lake and island, its liliputian summer-house, walks, and winding ways. We made but a hasty breakfast, so great was our eagerness to be off, and directly after it we started on our pilgrimage to the temple and mausoleum of Iyamitsu. There are only two temples and two mausoleums at Nikko, but they are more beautiful than all the other temples in Japan put together, and would more than repay the traveller for the long journey, even though he saw nothing else in the country.

Shogun Iyayasu was the founder of Tokyo, and was in the height of his power as military ruler when the country which he governed was in the golden age of her artistic life. He was the first Shogun to be buried at Nikko, and his grandson Iyamitsu was the only other to achieve a like distinction. To beautify the temples and burial-places of these two great warriors, all that there was of richest and rarest in Japan was showered upon them, and the genius and talent of the greatest artists and arti-

AVENUE AT NIKKO

sans were called forth to dispose these treasures suitably, and the result is certainly a dream of beauty.

On starting out, one of the party was carried in a kind of throne mounted on poles, and borne on the shoulders of four men, while the rest of us made our way on foot. The way to the tomb of Iyamitsu, which, as it was the less gorgeous of the two, was visited first, is up a flight of shallow, moss-covered stone steps, shaded by huge cryptomerias and maples, and ending at a broad plateau surrounded by temples. From this plateau starts the famous avenue of cryptomerias, which was formerly the royal road to Nikko, which goes straight as an arrow to Imachi, twelve miles away, and is lined on either side by superb trees. Having waited a moment to regain our breath, and to allow our queen to descend from her throne, we passed through a carved gateway into the lower court of the temple. At the right was a carved and gilded pavilion. Under this was a square basin of stone, into which water, cold as ice and clear as crystal, flowed from the mouth of a bronze dragon. So exact is the hollowing out of this basin that the water overflows all four sides with absolute evenness, and one feels as though gazing at a solid block of marble. Having drunk at this sacred fountain, we turned and ascended the lichen-covered, fern-fringed stone steps which are at the left of the court, and after several turns found ourselves at the doorway of the temple. It is absolutely impossible to give in detail the beauties of this building. I do not believe that a person exists who could convey in words an adequate idea of its beauties. When the present Emperor came to the throne, and Shintoism became the national religion, he removed from the other and larger temple all the symbols of the Buddhist faith, substituting in their stead the meaningless round mirror and paper-topped sticks of Shintoism. But the temple of Iyamitsu was spared, and there remain in all their glory the superb lacquer boxes, the silk-bound drums, the gongs, the brass and silver flags, the huge gilt lotus blossoms in their bronze vases, the tall stork and turtle candlesticks, the gold, brass, bronze and red, all the panoply and trappings used by the grand old worshippers of Buddha. Here are found scattered with unsparing hand old cloisonné, the art of making which is lost forever, gold lacquer worth many times its own weight, paintings and carvings by masters of the arts, silks and brocades laboriously woven and embroidered by hand, rare metals and precious stones, fashioned by cunning fingers into shapes of imperishable beauty. Riches succeed riches, until one emerges at last dazed and bewildered, and glad to rest the eye upon the soft greens and grays of the courtyard. The tomb of Iyamitsu stands in a cryptomeria grove above the temple, and is extremely simple and plain.

From this spot we descended by a winding path to a temple, where a few discreetly bestowed coins enabled us to assist at a Shinto service and dance. With much solemnity we were conducted to a row of chairs at the right of the altar. The latter consists of a low square table on which rest the sacred mirror (a round disk of polished brass), flanked on either side by a brass vase, one containing a plain wooden wand, the other a bunch of paper fastened to a silk-covered stick. The four sides of the temple were, as usual, open to the winds of heaven. The officiating priests were two, attired alike in green

TEMPLE STEPS.

and blue robes, and tall conical caps of brown. They
were assisted by a priestess, who was dressed in an under-garment of red silk, over which fell a robe of finest
white crêpe embroidered with wistaria, and who had a
sort of white crêpe handkerchief picturesquely tied over
her satiny black hair. When we were finally seated the
second priest squatted in front of an oblong drum and
began to beat slowly. At the sound, the head priest
emerged from behind a curtain hanging at the side of
the altar, knelt before the mirror, bowed, clapped his
hands, and rolled out a long and sonorous prayer : then
he arose, took the paper-fringed stick, and turning toward
us waved it over our heads. This our guide told us was
to purify us and make us worthy of witnessing the rest
of the ceremony. Then came more bowing and prayers,
at the conclusion of which the head-priest retired to a
place by the side of his subordinate, and the priestess came
forward. She held in one hand a long black wand, and
in the other a sort of magnified baby's rattle of silver.
The sacred dance consisted of slow steps backward and
forward, stately bows to right and left, and many pros-

strations before the altar. accompanied by the sharp
jingle of the rattle and the monotonous roll of the drum.
Having finished, the priestess retired to her cushion, and
the head priest rising, beckoned us to follow him. We
crossed a narrow passage, went up some narrow steps,
and then were required to kneel before an inner shrine.
There the priest reverently uncovered to our view a
small silver snake. representing the patron saint : gave
us sacred *saké* from a sacred bowl, and insisted upon our
nibbling at a sacred cake. Then he waved his hands
over us. praying all the gods to give us long life and
happiness : we slowly arose to our feet and the ceremony
was over.

It was well that a night intervened between our visits
to the two great temples, for to see them both in one
day would be too much for any mind to absorb and
digest.

The approaches to the two are much alike. and both
have stone-paved courtyards in front of them. But it
would take weeks and months of constant study to master
all that there is to be seen of their beauty. The court

leading to the temple of Iyayasu is enclosed by a wooden wall, every inch of which is carved and painted, and having in its centre a gateway which might well be termed the eighth wonder of the world, so exquisitely is it wrought. At one side of this gateway is a piece of carving purposely inserted upside down, the builder having a superstitious fear that a work so perfect would call down the wrath of the gods. This temple, as I have said, has been shorn of its Buddhist beauties, but enough remains in the way of carving, painting, etc., to make it a never-forgotten vision of beauty. Gateways, carvings, gold, silver, bronze and lacquer, brocade and embroidery, cloisonné, and satsuma, stone, and bronze lanterns, moss-covered stairway hung with fringes of dew-gemmed ferns, lofty torii of copper and gilt, succeeded each other in swift succession, until we were fain to cry " Hold : enough ! the mind and brain can stand no more."

And then we turned aside from all this magnificence, and made our way up the mossy stairway to the quiet grove, where lie the mortal remains of the man for whom all this beauty came into being. Iyayasu's ashes

CHILDREN'S MATSURI

rest in a plain bronze cenotaph, inscribed with his name
in brass characters. An incense burner and two tall
stork candlesticks stand in front of it. a solid stone
fence surrounds it, and it is guarded on all sides by those
tall and stately sentinels, the cryptomerias. The soft
rustle of their swaying branches, the startled cry of a
rook, the distant murmur of some mountain torrent, are
the only sounds that break the stillness. It is a strange
and solemn silence which enfolds the resting-place of
that grand old soldier, who must sleep sweetly here after
the battles and bloodshed of his busy life.

We left Nikko most reluctantly after a stay of only
three days, where we could have gladly spent as many
weeks, and returned to Yokohama with only a week before us in which to complete our final preparations for
departure. The last few days were hurried—chaotic—a
whirl of last things, bills, farewell calls, and packing,
and then came the very last day of all—the last 'rikisha
race down the Bund, so strange to us three months ago,
and now as familiar as the best-known sight at home,
the hurried embarkation on the tug, the puffing and bust-

ling out to the great white Empress, riding at her anchorage amid-stream.

Many of our friends were there to see us off, and our cabins were redolent with flowers. A short hour of farewells ensued, then came the signal " All ashore," the last strong hand-clasps from those we had grown to know and like so well, then the screw turned—slowly at first, then at full speed, and as twilight fell the last shadowy outlines of beautiful Fujiyama melted imperceptibly into the soft clouds, and with eyes half filled with regretful tears we said *sayonara* to Japan.

www.ingramcontent.com/pod-product-compliance
Lightning Source LLC
Chambersburg PA
CBHW032102010726
47493CB00008B/2503